Slowly We Rise

The Different Stroke

Table of Contents

CHAPTER ONE

BANCROFT HOUSEHOLD

Hank stared at the phone in disbelief for a moment, then took a few deep breaths to calm himself. There was no need to panic; there were a ton of people at the DMV, and by Floyd's glee when he got out of the car only an idiot would be unable to deduce that he had passed the test. And there were dozens upon dozens of people at church who saw Floyd and Theo bickering. Even if no one there was directly connected to Harmon...

No, stop being paranoid. I can barely take a piss without it being reported in the papers the next day.

It was okay.

If not, it would be okay.

Everything had to be okay, because he didn't know what to do if it wasn't.

His heart dropped when he saw an incoming call from Avery.

"What's up, you guys okay?"

Avery sounded embarrassed. "We're okay, but Floyd saw Daven's truck in his driveway and pulled in behind it. He got up to the front door before I could figure out a reason to stop him."

Hank had to almost restrain himself from throwing the phone to the ground in frustration.

"I see. Guessing he wants to tell his Uncle Dav he just got his license. What's he doing?"

"Yes, telling him about the license. I'm with them on the porch. Now Floyd is asking why he's not at work." Avery's voice was very low, he must be standing within a few feet of them.

"Fuck me…I should have thought of that. I'm sorry." At least it was an enclosed porch and no one could take pictures of them. "If it gets awkward, go up and tell him his dad wants him home right away. Be nice, don't give anything away. I haven't told him anything."

"Yes, sir. See you soon."

"You sick, Uncle Dav? If you need some DayQuil or something, we have some at the house."

"No, it's okay, Floyd. Thanks, though."

"Are you growing a beard..?"

Daven smiled. "I was going to because I've never had one before, but it's all scratchy and itchy. Definitely not for me. I don't know how your dad can stand it."

He caught a glance at Avery as the man hung up the phone. There was absolutely no need to explain the look he threw him; they knew each other so well that speech was usually unnecessary for communication.

Daven's ruffled Floyd's hair, then nodded at Avery. "I think your dad wants you home."

Avery nodded. "He does, Floyd. I'm sorry. He's got to go back to work now."

"Come here. Hug," said Daven as he held out his arms. "I'm so proud of you, Floyd-o." He held him much tighter than usual, longer than he normally did, and when they parted his eyes were maybe a little wet.

"Uncle Dav, I...are you sure you're okay? I know Dad hasn't been very nice to you. He's been really bent out of shape la-"

"Let's go, Floyd," said Avery firmly. "Time's up."

"Wait a minute," Floyd responded without looking at him, and quite rudely. Avery blinked; Floyd had never defied him before. "Can I come in and pet Shannon?" Daven's golden retriever, much beloved by the Bancroft family, especially Theo.

Avery stepped forward and put his hand on Floyd's shoulder, and Floyd shook it off as if were a wasp with the stinger deployed. "I said wait!" he shrieked, and Daven stepped in at this point.

"*Floyd* . You got to go. Shannon will be here when you return. She's asleep now, anyway."

Two sudden loud barks from within the house immediately refuted this declaration, and Floyd's expression fell as he realized he wasn't welcome.

"Okay. I get it. Sorry I bothered you." He turned away dejectedly, and Avery placed a hand on his shoulder.

"Don't touch me!" Floyd shrieked again as he violently slapped the man's hand away, shoved him, and hurried off.

Avery turned and looked at his friend with a shocked and apologetic expression.

"It's okay, Avery, not your fault," Daven offered quickly, his voice rougher than usual.

"I'm so sorry about all this, Daven. I really am. I'm sure Hank will come around and we'll get back to normal soon."

"Thanks, but I would advise you not to share that opinion with anyone else. If Hank learns you're sympathetic to me, well...it won't be pretty. You can pretend you hate me, it's ok."

"I don't, and I never will. And I'm sure of that without even knowing what's going on. See you soon, Daven."

"Later, crocodile."

"Alligator."

"What?"

"It's later, *alligator*. In a while, crocodile."

"Oh. Noted." Daven's demeanor was serene, but Avery could swear he detected a trace of sudden amusement as Daven's attention was diverted to the driveway. "Oh, look. There goes Floyd, you better catch him."

Avery cursed as Floyd started up the Thunderbird and peeled out across Daven's beautiful front lawn. Then he jumped into SUV and put the pedal to the metal, but he had the courtesy to back up into the street first instead of tearing up the grass. He tailed Floyd closely all the way home, intercepted him in the garage, then took an inescapable grip on the boy's arm and marched him into the house.

Hank lasted all of five minutes after the call before he gave in and tore into the envelope Daven had sent. There was a handwritten note paper-clipped on the top, in Daven's neat handwriting.

Hank -

I realize that by the time you read this, our friendship will have come to an end - even if our work partnership doesn't. If you fired me, it was likely a bitter and painful conversation that I rightfully deserved, and you should feel no guilt or shame in enacting that resolution. My deepest regret is that my actions were wholly inexcusable and forced you into an impossible situation. Regardless of what you may think of me now, or whether I am to retain the honor of being your employee, please know that I believe in you 100% and will continue to fight for what we have always believed in....even if I have to do it alone.

Daven

PS

Please shred this note after reading.

Hank threw the letter down on the desk and wiped his eyes, fighting back anger and sadness and an overwhelming desire to forgive and forget and throttle and yell and apologize and..

God damn you, Daven.

There was a loud thump and a few whirs from the back wall of his office indicating that the garage door was opening. *Not now. Has it been ten minutes already? I'm losing track of time. I'm losing track of everything.*

Was it even still Monday? It felt like weeks had passed since his confrontation with his best friend less than 24 hours ago. He could still hide in his study for a little while, anyway. It was only 2:30pm and Avery knew never to bother him, that he would come out only when he was ready. Avery would just have to wait patiently, and allow more than enough time for Hank to pull himself together.

Except that today was different. There was a firm knock on his study door.

"It's Avery. May I speak with you, please?"

Hank looked up in confusion. Avery had never once knocked on his study door before. Nobody ever had, come to think of it.

"What is it?"

"I have Floyd with me, and we have a situation."

Good god. What else could possibly go wrong with this shit show of a week?

"Come in," he answered resignedly, his annoyance turning to shock as he saw the obviously strong grip Avery had on his son.

"Stand still," growled Avery as he released Floyd. Again, Hank was shocked. His guards were not authorized to handle his children in this manner, period, so what he was seeing definitely raised his hackles.

"What's going on?" he asked in a neutral tone, eyeing Floyd's defiant expression and trying not to jump to conclusions. Whatever Avery did, it was unfailingly for a very good reason.

Avery spoke calmly and without inflection. "Floyd fought me as I tried to lead him away from Daven, then drove across his lawn and tore it up...and then proceeded to drive along Olympic Avenue for five minutes before I forced him to turn around and come back."

"I'm sorry, but....is this a joke?" Hank asked after an extremely long and uncomfortable silence.

"No, sir," replied Avery, just as tense. "Several paparazzi were parked in front of Daven's, but they didn't follow us as far as I know."

"Oh, I'm sure they saw the whole damned thing," Hank said between his teeth. Floyd was dead. *So dead.*

Another long silence, and then Floyd blurted out, "Why aren't I allowed to talk to Uncle Dav all of a sudden? What did I do? Or what did he do?"

Hank was quite literally speechless for a few seconds, and then he responded coolly, "Don't change the subject. Did you really do what Avery has just described?"

"Yes," Floyd replied immediately. "Because he wouldn't let me talk to him, and then he grabbed me and-"

"I didn't grab him, sir. I barely put my hand on his shoulder to guide him away, and he shoved me and ran off."

"*Shoved*? I barely even touched you-"

"Alright, stop. Both of you." Hank felt like his head was going to implode and explode at the same time, not that such a thing was possible. "Floyd, stay here. Avery, come with me for a moment."

Hank stalked out of the study with Avery close on his heels, and they went into the kitchen.

"Avery, for god's sake. What the hell is this?"

"Exactly what I said, sir. No exaggeration. If anything, I'm downplaying it. And he tried to get away from me again when we got back, that's why I was holding on to him." He stared back at Hank unblinkingly. Undefiantly. Unemotionally. "Can I speak freely?" he added after a moment.

"Yes."

"Don't be mad at me, because it has to be said. You know how deeply he's attached to Daven. I don't want to be in the middle again if you're going to keep them apart. He hates me right now, and we can't have that long-term. Just my two cents, Hank."

And you're exactly right, Hank mused, even as he acknowledged to himself (again) that he was irked about Floyd idolizing Daven so much.

"I hear you, Avery. Thank you. You said Floyd fought you? Explain exactly what happened, please. Every detail. And please know that I'm not upset with you."

Floyd was gone when Hank returned back to the study a few minutes later.

Yep. Dead. Even more dead now, if possible.

He rubbed his temples for a minute or two, talked soothingly out loud to keep himself from screaming, and then looked around his desk. The memo from Daven was still inside the FedEx envelope untouched, but the handwritten letter was in a different position than where he left it. And it was face up. He had set it face down.

He was puzzled for a moment, and then he realized Floyd had read the letter in the past few minutes. *Shit.* It was already 3pm, and Hank really didn't have time for this. He trudged upstairs to Floyd's room, where he found his son listening to music with his gigantic headphones firmly encasing his ears. He was sitting on his bed against the headboard, arms crossed, looking straight ahead at the wall.

Hank strode over and pulled the headphone cord out of the stereo, then took the headphones off. Floyd did nothing.

"Hey," Hank snapped. "Look at me."

Floyd closed his eyes and leaned his head back as if he was relaxing, but Hank could see every muscle tensed up like they were clamping down on his bones.

"Nobody is keeping you from Daven. You jumped to conclusions and-"

Now Floyd turned to look at him, eyes blazing. "I read his letter. You aren't even friends anymore, dad, so don't give me that bullshit."

Before Hank could stop himself, he slapped Floyd full across the face, hard. Then he backed up as Floyd lifted a hand to his cheek and stared at his dad with eyes wider than they had ever been. Shock. Hurt, too, but mostly shock and perhaps a little bit of incomprehension about what had just occurred. His dad had never slapped him or Theo before, nor even threatened it.

"Go to the spare room and wait for me there. I'll be home around seven. If you're not up in three seconds..."

Floyd jumped up, still clasping a hand to his cheek. His eyes were wet and it was only a matter of seconds before the floodgates opened. Hank didn't want to see that, so he left the room and trusted Floyd to do what he was told. Mostly because he had no idea what the hell to do if he didn't.

Hank quickly descended the stairs towards his study to grab his briefcase. "Avery!" he shouted down the other staircase that led to the basement. "Let's head back to the office."

Maurice and the housekeeper were waiting by the door, and now Hank turned to his jumpy butler. "If Floyd doesn't go into the spare room within five minutes, let a guard know to call me. That's all I'm going to say, clear?"

"Yes, sir," said Maurice, his expression clearly indicating he was dying to know what was up. He was, by far, the biggest gossip in the household. Since by law all indentured house servants were unpaid and allowed no material belongings, there was very little else to do but talk amongst themselves, and their imaginations were boundless. That was why Hank never told him much, and why he spent most of his time in his study.

As Hank walked out the front door, Lucas, Brittany and Theo were coming in.

"Hey, Theody," Hank said, enveloping his youngest in an obviously unwanted embrace. "How was the...the...." He realized he still didn't know where his youngest had been all day.

"Fine."

Hank knew that was all he was going to get for now. Theo was stiff as a board, obviously still hostile and distant after being paddled yesterday, so Hank released him and let him go on his way. It would be at least another day before he would look at his dad, never mind engage with him in a voluntary act of affection.

Hank gave up on him and got into the car, dialing Taylor at the same time.

"Hey Hank, I was just about to call you. We got a fax from Harmon at 3."

"Thank god. Finally a piece of good news today."

Taylor took a deep breath. "Not really. I'm sorry, Hank."

"Sorry for what?" Hank asked in a confused tone.

"The fax we got back...it was the form, but it's not completed. Harmon wrote on it instead, and it says...wait, first you have to promise you won't shoot the messenger."

"Promise. What does it say?" Hank demanded.

"It says... *Your request is refused. Please find below a statement which will be released to the press at 4:30pm, should you choose to pursue the matter any further. - Harmon*"

"Holy fucking shit," muttered Hank, absolutely astonished at this turn of events. "Dare I ask you to read me the statement?"

"No."

"Read it anyway."

Sigh. "Here goes: *At 3:45pm Pacific Time / 4:45 Mountain time, we were obliged to notify the FBI of a blackmail attempt made at 12:40pm PST today by Hank Bancroft, Leader of the Seditionists Party, in regards to surveillance tapes seized from their office in Greeley, CO. Details as to the nature of the attempt will remain confidential until such time as the investigation is complete.*"

Hank seriously felt like asking Avery to drive the SUV off the side of the cliff they were currently skirting. Just a few seconds of terror, and it would all be over. He wouldn't have to deal with this, or with Daven. Or Rupert. Or with Floyd, or Theo. Or the dead woman, or the mysterious caller. A quick but messy death would solve it all...

"Hank, I'm sorry. I don't even know what to say."

"Alright. So...it says at 3:45 they notified the FBI. It's only 3:02 right now, which means they haven't actually done it yet. Right? You're sure it says 3:45?"

"Yes, positive. That's strange, maybe a typo?"

Hank smirked. "I'm going to call Harmon and wave the white flag. Put the fax on my desk and lock the door to my office."

"Wait, Hank-"

Hank hung up and dialed Harmon, and told him he was backing off and to not contact the FBI or issue the press release. Hank hated the smugness in the man's voice as he agreed to "cancel the premature press release" due to a "simple misunderstanding." Hank hated groveling and acting like he'd lost a battle, but gritted his teeth and got through it. The reward would come soon.

Avery dropped him at the back door of the building, and Hank raced to his office faster than he ever had in his life. Feeling rather silly, he said a prayer while dialing Stewart, deputy director of political affairs at the FBI.

The man picked up the call on the first ring. Thank god.

"Stewart? Hank Bancroft here. Before I say anything else, please note it is currently 3:10pm Pacific time, 4:10pm Mountain Time. Is this call being recorded?"

"Of course," replied Stewart, his tone indicating how puzzled he was by the urgency in Hank Bancroft's tone. "What's going on, Mr. Bancroft?'

"Have you spoken to Harmon today regarding the surveillance tapes from Greeley?"

"No, last talked to him yesterday. Why?"

"Nobody from the party has contacted you today in regards to the tapes from Greeley, or to speak about my role in requesting the tapes from you at the same time they are

released to the Urbanes? No contact at all? Please confirm
with a yes or no.”

“No. Nothing.”

“Then I need your fax number, immediately. Please. One that
goes straight to you.”

“Yeah, the one on my desk.” He gave the number.

Hank smiled and carefully placed Harmon’s fax back into the
sending tray, punching in Stewart’s number and hitting
transmit.

“Let me know when you get it.”

“Okay. It’s coming. You mind telling me what’s going on?”

“Harmon just tried to blackmail me in order to impede a
murder investigation, and I’ve got it all in his very own
writing.”

CHAPTER TWO

Seditionists Headquarters, Los Angeles

Monday, December 27

4:00 pm

"Hey. So Floyd tells me you're growing a beard. Couldn't believe it unless I heard it from the man himself."

Daven furrowed his eyebrows. "That's...that's what you're calling me about?"

Hank had to resist the urge to laugh. "No, Dav, it's not what I'm calling about. That was an attempt to break the ice."

"Right. It's actually just two days of stubble. If you're calling about the grass, it's okay. There's no permanent damage."

"No...I'm calling because Avery pretty much called me a dick for what happened between you and Floyd. I shouldn't have put him in the middle, and now I want you to understand something. My intentions were good. I was only trying to prevent awkwardness for you, from Floyd asking too many questions and saying too much. You know how he can be."

"Yes. Gets that from his father."

Hank rolled his eyes. It wasn't the first time they've had the same exchange, so he kept going without acknowledging it. "My point is that I have no intention of not letting him see you. It's just that the timing was really damned awkward, and...well, you should also know that afterwards he went snooping through my mail and saw the note you wrote me. Which, by the way, was very kind. Thank you for that."

Silence.

"At any rate," Hank continued, feeling horribly off-kilter by this stilted and one-sided conversation, "I think that I need to tell him something ASAP, and I want you to think about it and let me know what you would like me to say. I'm afraid that if I do it on my own I'll villainize you, and that's the last thing I want. I'll be home at seven. Call me before then."

Damn it, Hank. Stop giving him orders. He's not your employee right now.

"Take him to the press conference," Daven finally said.

"What?" Hank thought he hadn't heard correctly.

"Take him to the press conference. Let him hear the story from the calm, honest, unemotional Hank Bancroft, rather than the angry father who can't seem to ever discuss things objectively with his sons. Let him make up his own mind for once."

Hank was a bit set back on his heels by that; it was the first time Daven had ever criticized his parenting.

"I...wow. Okay. I'll think about it."

"How is he doing otherwise?"

Hank didn't want to say it, but he really needed someone to talk to. "To be honest, Dav, I haven't spent enough time with the boys and sometimes feel like they are strangers in my house. They're growing up too fast and leaving me behind...I'm sorry, I don't mean to dump this on you. I only called to apologize for having Avery step in like he did."

"I forgive you. And you should forgive Floyd, too. Completely and entirely, no caveats."

"Why would I do that?"

"Because he won't forget it. I should go, Hank. You have to talk to the world in an hour."

Yes, but the only person in the world I want to talk to is you…

"Thanks, Dav. Let's chat again soon."

"Sure. Good luck with the press conference. Stay true."

Those two words were always that last thing Daven said to him before any of Hank's public speaking events: Stay true.

Lump, meet throat.

It took Hank a few moments to lay the receiver back on the hook, as lost in thought as he was. Daven had been incredibly candid all of a sudden, which was strangely intriguing. Not the black and white strategist now that he didn't have a job to do. He should open up more often. It was rather…refreshing, even if he did insult him once. Or was it twice?

Hank picked up the phone and called the house.

"Brittany, have Floyd get dressed in his nicest suit and bring him to the office. Tell him he's not in trouble. You'll have to hurry. Thanks."

Taylor poked her head into Hank's office. "Hank, you have a visitor. Really handsome dude, too. Best keep him away from the secretaries."

Hank looked up and waved his hand. "Thanks. Come in, Floyd. Close the door."

Floyd had flushed at Taylor's words, but now he looked as though now he was the one about to get fired from a job. He stood by the door, somewhat petrified, and stared around the office through the glass panel in the wall. He had never been there during the day, and was a bit dazzled by all the activity.

"Floyd. Sit. You're not in trouble. Relax. Grab a water from the fridge if you want."

Hank continued writing out his thoughts on top of the press release as his son declined the water invitation and slowly lowered himself into one of the "electric chairs," as some people called them. He rarely had anyone in his office unless they were in trouble; he much preferred to go around and hang out elsewhere to talk and meet. Especially Daven's office because of that ridiculous fluffy chair that Rupert loved so much. When they all met together, though, the boss always got the chair. Period.

Hank set his pen down and leaned over to grab two bottles of water from his refrigerator, handing one to Floyd.

"Here. Take it with you."

"Take it where?" asked Floyd in confusion. He looked as if he expected to be slapped again.

Hank sat back in his chair and downed half a bottle of water. "To the press conference. I have to talk fast now. The reason I made you leave Daven's house is because I had to suspend him from his job for 30 days. I hadn't told you yet because it just happened. Floyd, I want you to remember that no matter what is said today, Dav is still Dav and always will be. He didn't break the law, just a company policy. Yes, I'm angry with him right now, but my greatest hope is that I will regain my friendship with him after this is over."

Floyd wasn't really comprehending Hank's reasoning at first. "But why am I here?"

"Because your Uncle Dav wanted you to be. Okay?"

Floyd seemed to not understand still, but he nodded. "Okay. Is he here, too?"

"No, but I'm here and will do everything I can to protect his reputation. He means everything to me - to us - but when people screw up this big...it can get really ugly. Maybe even for a long time. I'll need your cooperation and support to help get through this. Do you understand?"

"Yes, sir."

"Okay. You're just here to listen and learn. You can ask me any questions you'd like afterwards at home, although I probably can't answer them."

"Afterwards? You mean, before or after you...*you know...*"
Again with the fearful expression.

Hank softened his tone considerably as he set his water bottle down and leaned across the desk. "I'm not going to *do* anything, Floyd. You're completely forgiven...by me, at least. You still need to apologize to Dav and Avery, though."

Floyd looked flabbergasted. "But I don't...why are you..."

Because Daven said so.

"Because I said so. I'm out of time now. Go with Taylor and she'll seat you in the briefing room. Remember you're just there to listen, do not speak with anyone about anything. And most like there will be cameras on you, so don't be picking your nose or anything like that."

That comment, and Hank's unexpected forgiveness, finally broke Floyd out of his shell. He smiled a little and then grabbed the bottle of water. "Does that mean I can't fart, either?"

Hank chuckled. "The microphones are all up with me, so you're safe to fart away. Just make sure you're sitting in between two Urbanes when you do it."

CHAPTER THREE

For whatever reason, Hank never got nervous before or during press conferences. Considering it had recently become a class 2 felony offense for party officers and government employees to lie outright while in the course of their duties, such a public gathering should make anybody nervous. But he liked to theorize it didn't matter; that his lifelong and sincere desire to be honest and transparent soothed his conscience so much that speaking to this room of a hundred people came just as naturally as speaking to anyone else. So when Taylor was working with the A/V guys to do the sound test, he calmly re-read his notes behind the little screen in the corner and waited for the doors to open. Calm as can be. Everything was fine. He had this.

Then the room began to fill up and he recognized some prominent Urbanes at the exact same time he suddenly remembered he had told Floyd that Janet was a double agent. And then, heart racing, he spotted Floyd, chatting animatedly in the corner with one of the most nosy and manipulative reporters the world had ever known. One of Harmon's favorites, actually.

"Taylor!" he hissed. "Floyd's with Hailey. Why aren't you with him?"

"You said to sit him down and-"

"Get him, *now* . Bring him here."

"Okay, sorry." She ran off, and Hank sweated bullets in the horrifying moments it took her to pull his son away from the vile woman. Was it too late? Who knew how long they'd been chatting. Did she corner him outside the doors for the past 15 minutes? Surely Brittany would have pulled him away from her, if so. Where the hell *was* Brittany, anyway?

Floyd suddenly appeared behind the screen, looking scared. "What's wrong, dad?"

Hank took his arm angrily and pulled him further back, so that they were both leaning against the wall and out of sight. "I specifically told you that you were only here to listen, and not talk. That woman you were just chatting with? Basically my worst enemy. What were you saying to her?"

"Ow, dad. Let go, please." Hank did, then Floyd continued, "I was telling her that I was only here to listen and learn, and that I wasn't authorized to speak with anyone but you."

Hank looked at him sideways. "It looked like more than that."

"It wasn't! I had to say it twice. She's so nosy. Then she was congratulating me on my license, so I was just saying thank you and how excited I was to drive. That's all!"

"Hank, 5pm. You're on," busted in Taylor, in that overtly bossy tone that meant Hank was about to make a fool of himself if he didn't do what she said.

"Wait," said Hank and she stopped in her tracks. "Take Floyd to the back corner away from Hailey. Both of you stand there the entire time, do not move...and Floyd? Play deaf if anyone else asks you anything. Not a word. If I see you open your mouth even once-"

" *Okay* ! I got it." He caught Hank's expression and then straightened up. "I mean. Yes, sir."

"Go."

"Aye aye, captain!" That was from Taylor this time, eye roll included. He would have to chat to her about that later. Amazing strategist or not, she tended to be insolent at the worst possible moments. It was especially unwise to do it in front of his very impressionable son.

Hank breathed in deeply and stepped out from behind the screen while the cameras clicked approximately five thousand times. For the hundredth time he idly wondered how many photographers it would take to change a light bulb...

"Good evening. Thank you for joining me." Lighting setups for live broadcasts were always blinding, so he took the opportunity to squint like he was adjusting his eyes in order to watch Taylor and Floyd take up station in the far back corner. There was Brittany, too. Good, although he would be chatting with her later for leaving his son alone with Hailey.

His throat swelled a little after he had automatically looked for Rupert and Daven in the opposite corner, where they always stood, talking together and making notes. Sometimes Rupe would make an obscene gesture at Hank if he said something he shouldn't, or to loosen him up or distract him if he started getting twitchy with the reporters.

Hank knew his audience had always really been his two favorite aides, not the reporters. They were a happy little trio. Now, though, his attention was on...Hailey. All he could think about was Hailey. And how Floyd knew something he shouldn't, and had been talking to her.

And now, for the first time ever, he was completely petrified in front of those microphones and learning really quickly what it was like to feel stage fright. He'd had no idea how much those two men carried him through these moments, and their absence was nearly unbearable.

Come on, Hank. You've got this.

"Ahem. I will begin by reading the statement that was released this morning." He proceeded to read it, but didn't really hear his own words. Why the hell did he tell Floyd about Janet, for god's sake? Oh, that's right. Because Floyd was having a temper tantrum, and you were weak in handling it. *You're weak in handling everything lately.*

"At this point I have nothing to add to the statement, but I will take ten questions now."

In order to avoid bias, he never selected the reporters himself for questions. Upon entering the room, every single reporter chose a numbered clicker from a basket, and there was a green light behind him on the little stage activated by a button he pushed on the podium when he was ready to take another question. The first person to click while it was green had their number pop up on an electronic signboard on the back wall for him to call out.

"Yes, number 47?"

An Seditionist, but an annoying one who pushed all the wrong buttons.

"Mr. Bancroft, regarding these bungled communications. Was there any confidential information that was compromised as a result of this violated policy?"

Bungled?? Go fuck yourself. "No. They would not have a job right now if that was the case. Hence the 'mitigating circumstances' I mentioned. Yes, number 13?"

Hailey, who was usually first to pull the trigger and get on the board. "Your statement says explicitly that you hold all your employees to equal and fair standards, so can you explain why Mr. Johansson received a heavier penalty than Mr. Aster?"

Hank almost laughed, because he had already predicted that would be her question as soon as he saw her in the lobby an hour ago. Everyone knew she harbored a secret crush on Daven...except Daven.

"He made two mistakes, and Rupert made one. I will not elaborate any further." Button press. "Yes, number 4?"

Another tough Urbane. "It seems odd that your two top executives would violate any policy at all, considering you've mentioned before that the three of you wrote them together and all of you have been with the party since day one. Was this violation entirely unintentional somehow, or was it blatant and purposeful?"

Shit. Although Hank had prepared an answer for this question, he was really hoping not to get it. There was an option to decline to answer, and he'd done so numerous times in the past if wasn't legally able to answer. Maybe he should refuse to take any questions at all in the first place, like Harmon always did, but then again...he was Hank Bancroft. Mr. Transparent. Mr. Cool. He *had* to answer.

It was easy to picture Rupert having an anxiety attack in the corner while he picked up his bottle of water to buy time to think some more, praying that whatever he said would be good enough to save his friend's careers. He knew Rupe and Dav were watching right now, from their homes. Waiting for him to give them hope...or to put the nail in the coffin.

Even worse, maybe they didn't care anymore and were looking for new jobs already.

"Right. Difficult but reasonable question. You know I don't spin things, as much as that would help sometimes, but I'm perfectly aware that this answer will sound like spin. And that's the only reason I'll admit that I'm uncomfortable with it. Yes, they both knowingly violated the policy. It was a difficult situation, and to be perfectly honest, I'm still struggling with my decision to suspend them because I still wonder what I would have done in their place. It's very likely I would have done the same thing. I don't know. There isn't an easy answer. Policies may be written in black and white, but reality isn't. As I said, there were mitigating circumstances. Moving on. Yes, number 98?"

Another no-nonsense Urbane. Great. And then another. Then a softball from an Seditionist. Then, *finally* ...the question he had been hoping for all along, from Harmon's other favorite weasel.

"I can take one more question, Yes, number 50."

The man stood up, looking more smug than usual. "On December 25 there was a murder of an Urbane employee on

Seditionists property in Colorado. Both parties have been strangely silent on the matter. Was this incident related the suspensions? Please give us an update as to how that investigation is going, and whether or not you are cooperating with Harmon in order to identify the attacker."

The room murmured in approval of the question.

Here goes nothing, he thought to himself. "That was actually three questions, maybe four, but I will answer anyway. First, the incidents with Rupert and Daven are entirely unrelated to the death on our property. Secondly, I have been in regular contact with both Harmon and the FBI with requests to have the surveillance tapes released to us. Unfortunately, I've been unsuccessful so far. I feel strongly, of course, that all three parties should work together and solve the crime as soon as possible in order to provide answers to Janet's family, but I cannot do that without the tapes."

He reached for his water bottle and took a huge swig, knowing that he absolutely, definitely, undeniably should NOT say what he was about to say anyway. Something he had been practicing for an hour to make it sound as natural as possible. If Rupert was here he would likely kick him in the nuts afterwards a few times, and Hank wouldn't even be mad.

Deep breath. Steady. "Therefore, around 3:30pm today I called the deputy director of the FBI for his assistance. For transparency's sake I must admit that this backfired and resulted in me being officially reprimanded for threatening Harmon by saying I would bring his refusal to cooperate with me to public attention unless he signed the waiver to release the tapes. That was inappropriate, and I was instructed to wait silently for further information. Thank you all again for being here, and have a nice evening."

Urbanes HQ, Denver

"*What. The. Fuck,*" muttered Harmon in shock as he watched Hank Bancroft throw him under the bus on national television. He glanced at his aides to check their reactions. Umber, Colbert all wore similar stricken expressions, Colbert in particular.

"Boss, we need to put out a statement ASAP," said Umber in a quiet tone. "We're going to get murdered for this. No pun intended."

Harmon was expressionless, which - as everyone knew - meant he was in his most dangerous state. "Yes, get me a draft as quickly as you can. Everyone out, please."

They all rushed out, and Harmon turned down the volume on the television and watched the local news wrap-up the hour. In silence, no captions. He didn't need them. He knew what they were saying.

Hank Bancroft had won again. His capitulation to the fax earlier today had merely been an act. And Harmon had bought it...hook, line, and sinker.

Tap. Tap. Tap.

Rupert's House

"*What. The. Fuck,* " murmured Daven and Rupert in unison.

There was a long pause, and then Rupert said plainly as he threw up his hands in surrender, "I'm going to kill him. That's it. He's dead. But I need a beer first." He got up and went into the kitchen.

"Get me one, too," shouted Daven as he dropped his head into his hands.

————-

FBI Headquarters, Philadelphia

"What. The. Fuck."

Stewart stared open-mouthed at the monitor in his office for a good five minutes, then brought up his email to send a note to his boss in the Capitol.

He didn't need to, she had already beat him to it:

Stewart, please issue a mandatory in-person summons to Hank Bancroft. I'm available at 8am or 2pm on Wednesday. Let me know you got this.

-Salome

On it.

-Stewart

Thanks. I will summon Harmon, too, if he responds with anything that fans the flames. I'll call you if so. Go home soon.

-Salome

We might as well do it now. I would bet my life right now that he'll fire back with something even worse within the hour.

-Stewart

You're right. Prepare it now and then pull the trigger when I give the ok. Keep in touch.

-Salome

Will do.

Stewart hit send and picked up the phone to dial his Los Angeles courier.

CHAPTER FOUR

Floyd was very quiet in the car on the way home from the press conference.

Too quiet.

Way too quiet.

"What's wrong?" Hank finally asked after about ten minutes of total silence.

"Nothing," Floyd replied. Then he unbuckled his seat belt and started to move to the third row of the SUV.

"Hey," snapped Hank, pulling him back down into place. "Put your seatbelt back on. Stay put."

"It's a red light-"

"*Floyd,*" Hank warned calmly, with an unmistakable edge to his tone. He could see Avery's eyes focus on them in the rearview mirror.

Floyd threw him a look, but snapped the seatbelt back into the buckle and turned to stare out the window. It reminded Hank of the times he would always pout as a little boy when they passed by Disneyland on the way back and forth to their old office in Santa Ana.

"Where do you want to go for dinner to celebrate your license?" Hank asked after a minute, after his annoyance faded away.

"Nowhere."

"I'm not aware of a restaurant called Nowhere. Want to try someplace that actually exists?"

"I don't care."

"Should I tell you we need to have a chat when we get home?"

"Do whatever you want."

Avery's eyes were still on them, so Hank looked right back at him until he looked away. Hank felt absurdly self-conscious all of a sudden, so he dropped the subject when he felt his phone buzzing with a number he didn't recognize. But it was coming from Philadelphia, so he had to pick up.

"This is Hank Bancroft."

"Good evening Hank. This is Salome Danby, director of the Office of Political Integrity under President Rickon. This call is being recorded."

Oh shit. "Good evening," he responded as pleasantly as he could manage.

"Listen, Hank, in the morning you're going to get a summons to meet me and Stewart in Philadelphia on Wednesday. Normally I don't call to give a heads-up, but I wanted to give you advanced notice so you can arrange for your flights and child care. I would advise you to fly private and bring your lawyer."

Hank's throat constricted a little. "Will this...may I assume I can book a round trip?"

"Yes. I am free at 8am or 2pm on Wednesday and you'll probably be here for two hours. Once you receive the officials summons, I expect you to respond immediately with details of your flight arrangements."

"Yes, ma'am. I'll take the 2pm time slot. Thank you for the heads-up."

"I would also advise you to issue no further statements or make any public comments, whatever Harmon says or does at this point. But that's not a gag order and it's completely up to you to take my advice or not."

Her tone was utterly professional and smooth, with a trace of British accent. No indication of emotion at all. Hank wasn't sure if that made him feel worse, or better. He may have been less alarmed if she had screamed at him outright. Kind of like how he felt better when Floyd bitched at him instead of shutting him out.

He turned to look at his son, who was paying no attention to the call.

"Thank you, again. See you on Wednesday."

Then to Floyd, as he poked him hard in the side. "Hey. How do you feel about a little trip to Philadelphia to see Independence Hall?"

Floyd hesitated, and then turned around to stare at him. "That's random, dad."

"Yeah. I have a meeting there on Wednesday and don't see any reason why you and Theo can't come out and spend the day sightseeing."

The boy's eyes suddenly got really big, and he retreated into his shell a little again. "I do. Because everyone will be watching us. Taking pictures. Following us."

Hank nodded. "Yeah, Floyd. In case you haven't noticed, that's the life we've lived for ten years now."

"Well, I don't want it anymore. Take Theo, he enjoys all the attention."

"He's not speaking to me right now, either." Hank's phone buzzed again; a call from Rupert. He sent it to voicemail. "Look, I know it's been a long day. Let's go home and pack. We'll head to Philly in the late morning and go someplace historic for dinner. Near Valley Forge there's an old tavern that was used to store gunpowder during the-"

"I *said* I don't want to go," Floyd growled, throwing his dad a look of pure annoyance and...hatred? Was that really...could it be *hatred* ?

Hank was actually so taken aback by his hostility that he had no reply to make. Seconds later the big SUV pulled up to the front door, and Floyd leaped out and disappeared past Maurice inside the house in a flash.

Hank got out and nodded at Maurice, who was now holding the door for him. "Did Floyd just breeze by you without saying anything?" he asked the man.

"It's ok, sir, he was obviously upset."

"Yeah. On behalf of my son, I apologize for his rudeness." Hank's blood was up now. Indentured or not, all of his household staff deserved to be treated courteously. Floyd knew better. It was time to have a chat.

——

Rupert's House

"Damn. He sent me straight to voicemail," Rupe muttered as he tossed his phone onto the table.

"I don't know why you expected otherwise. You ever had Hank pick up when he knows he's pissed you off? Because I haven't."

"No. Never, actually."

Daven took a large swig of his beer. "Honestly, Rupe, I can't fathom what he was thinking by slandering Harmon like that on national television. He's out of his fucking mind."

Rupert smiled. "No. It's not slander if it's true. I would have agreed with you five minutes ago, but I've changed my mind. He knows exactly what he's doing. Wish I had half the stones he does and a quarter of his brains."

Daven stared at him for a moment in stunned silence. "Would you mind letting me in on the secret? It feels to me like he's deliberately sabotaging himself, so yes, in that regard he knows exactly what he's doing."

"Well, think about it. We know for certain that Harmon is refusing to cooperate with Janet's murder, no matter what he says next. Hank has written proof of it with that reprimand they issued him, and it's going to be published in the weekly FBI digest...is tomorrow Tuesday? Yes, so tomorrow. For the whole nation to read."

"The general public doesn't read that!"

"They don't need to, because the reporters do it for them. And Harmon's party? Janet is one of *theirs*. That's going to throw his constituents into a feeding frenzy because his lack of cooperation makes no sense at all. Why would he block an investigation of his own employee's murder? We should turn on Boswin News just to see what they're saying."

Daven shook his head. "No, you missed something. Janet was one of ours. The faster the investigation moves, the faster that's going to be revealed."

Again, Rupe smiled. "Exactly. This investigation is going to move forward at light speed now, and the faster we are going to be vindicated, because the public will realize that obviously we would not kill our *own agent* on our own property. Not to mention we certainly wouldn't push for a deeper investigation if we did kill her. So the blame will shift to Harmon, who has just been publicly shamed for trying to hinder the whole damn thing. He'll be public enemy number one at just the right time."

"Oh." Dav nodded slowly as the puzzle pieces all came crashing down on him in slow motion. " *Oh.* Holy shit."

"Not only *that*," continued Rupe, "but this takes the attention off of us. Meaning, you and me. Who do you think is going to be the big story tonight? Little us taking a couple of phone calls? I don't think so. We're old news already."

Daven thought about it some more, feeling a little drained now. "You think that he...that he planned all this from the beginning? This chain of events? Or did he just get lucky?"

Rupe laughed. "Are you kidding me? We are talking about *Hank Bancroft*, right? Absolutely planned down to the minute."

"Yeah. I guess you're right. Well, good thing it all worked out. Be right back, need some water. Want another beer?"

"No, I'm good."

Jesus Christ, breathed Daven, as he went back into Rupe's kitchen and rummaged through the refrigerator. His heart was beating strangely now, with a rhythm and power he never felt before. It wasn't remotely pleasant. Sickly, even. And why was that? It shouldn't be. His friend, his boss, just took the nation by storm in just fifteen minutes and rescued his party from a pending debacle. Getting a murder investigation to move faster was no small thing. Making the opposition look like shit, which they were? Priceless.

Yes, quite a feat. He should feel proud of the man. Should be admiring his mentor. Praising him.

But why wasn't he? Hank *was* brilliant in his handling of this. His mind worked in ways Daven could never even imagine.

Amazingly brilliant.

Maybe a little *too* brilliant.

Maybe a little *too* calculating.

But still brilliant, all the same.

And frighteningly dangerous.

And that was why he felt no joy. Daven shut his eyes to the sudden, very belated pains of realization that maybe he had underestimated exactly *how* dangerous Hank Bancroft could be with a mind like that.

He put the bottle of water back in the fridge and grabbed another beer instead.

Bancroft Manor

Hank left his secretary's office after arranging for a charter jet and hotel rooms in Philadelphia, then trudged up the stairs to Floyd's room. His head felt like it weighed 500 pounds right now, easily. How could it only be 6:30pm? This day seemed to have lasted a month already. The last thing he needed was yet another fight with Floyd.

Charter jets were expensive. Hank had a lot of money, yes, but he hated throwing that much away in just a matter of hours. He couldn't even imagine how much Harmon's own personal jet cost every year, but it had to seriously hurt.

When he pushed open the door to his oldest's room he was delighted to see an open suitcase on the bed that was already half-full. Hank walked in.

"I take it this means you changed your mind about Philadelphia?"

"Yes. Because I know Theody will want to go and I don't want to be left here alone."

"Good. But the packing will have to wait. Come with me, let's talk."

Floyd paused in folding a shirt and watched him fearfully. "Are you going to-"

"Nope. Said I wouldn't, and I won't. Let's go into my sitting room."

They went into the little square room off his top floor master suite and sunk into the comfy chairs. Floyd looked around in wonder; he had never actually been allowed on this floor before in the entire ten years they'd lived in the house. It was Hank's private sanctuary, and he chose it for this particular conversation because Daven's house was in full view from where Floyd was sitting.

Sure enough, that immediately prompted Floyd to start talking. "I need to apologize to Uncle Dav," he said softly.

"Yep."

"Do you think he's mad at me?"

"I know for sure he isn't, but that doesn't make your actions any less serious. When do you want to do it?"

Floyd ignored the question. "Dad, the press conference is really bothering me. I don't like the way that you answered some of the questions."

Hank was completely caught off guard by this unexpected statement. "What? Why?"

He shrugged, then pulled his knees up to his chest. "The last one. About Harmon."

Floyd was terrified of Harmon, for some reason. Hank never could find out why; they'd never met before and neither of the boys were allowed to watch regular television or read the political sections of the newspaper. They didn't even have access to the internet yet.

Hank softened his tone. "Should I regret taking you?"

"No, but I wish I hadn't been there. It was the first time I've seen you actually working, you know?"

"No it's not. You've seen me give interviews before."

"This was different."

"Why?"

Floyd looked away, towards Daven's house. "I don't know. It's just...you..."

Hank was fighting impatience now, but he did his best to hide it.

"What, Floyd? Talk to me."

"It's just...I didn't know how powerful you are until recently. How everybody listens to every word you say, and wants to know what you think about everything. They want to know everything about you, and me. When you freaked out on me for talking to that woman, it scared me when you called her your worst enemy. And the photographers, and the guards. How many enemies do you *have*, dad?"

The poor kid was almost beside himself with fear, and Hank's heart shattered into a million pieces. He resisted the urge to go pick Floyd up and put him in his lap.

"I understand where you're coming from. But I didn't mean *enemy* like she's trying to kill me or anything. She's a reporter, and she likes to gossip about me and try to embarrass me. They all do. She won't physically harm me. Or you. I shouldn't have used the word enemy. I'm really sorry that frightened you."

Floyd wasn't convinced. "Dad, I want you to quit your job so we can be a normal family."

"I see. Is that why you've been acting out so much lately? You do realize I've had to punish you more times in the past two months than in the last two years combined?"

"Yes. Because I'm scared."

"We have nine security guards who follow us hand and foot. Nothing has ever happened before, so why suddenly worry now? Don't be scared of Harmon."

Floyd stared out the window again, swallowed hard, then looked back at Hank. "I wasn't talking about Harmon. I was talking about you."

Hank's heart stopped for a moment. This was something he always suspected, but hoped to be wrong about. Even though he knew he wasn't. *Well. Now you know.*

Floyd was trembling. He had been doing that a lot lately, even when Hank wasn't even mad about anything. It had started in

November, after Hank belted him for the first time in months for snooping in his office and reading an old article about his involvement in bringing down the corrupt and morally bankrupt Democrat and Republican parties in the terrible years of the disastrous Durdan presidency. That day, Floyd learned that his father, Rupert, Daven, and even Harmon himself would be forever known as part of the hundreds of men and women who tore apart and then rebuilt the nation within two years: *The Seditionists.*

Unfortunately, this particular article had focused on Hank alone, due to an early infamous photo of him on the Capitol steps during Durdan's second inauguration ceremony. It was a dazzling, candid shot of him single-handedly stopping a violent protester with one hand while shooting the finger to the shocked president with the other hand. That photo had instantly become a symbol of the movement, and to Hank's utter horror he soon found his face (and finger) plastered all over posters, t-shirts, and protest signs. For *years.*

Floyd hadn't really been the same since learning his dad was the person in the iconic photo that sparked the Second American Revolution, and Hank really didn't know what the hell to do about it now. He had already explained that he wasn't a leader and was basically relegated to being a bored paper pusher after the image made it too dangerous for him to be out in public, but nothing registered. Floyd was too young to understand the politics of it all. He was only three years old when it all ended. A newborn when the picture was taken. But to him, and to millions of other youngsters as well, his dad *was* the revolution.

"Okay," Hank said, somehow finding the ability to swallow again. "Listen, why don't we call Uncle Dav and ask if you can come over and apologize to him and play with Shannon for a little while."

"He's not there. Wait, aren't you going to tell me to not be afraid of you?"

Hank got up to look out the window. No truck in the driveway. Probably with Rupert, drinking beer and talking about the press conference.

Talking about *him*.

Gently he sat back down directly across from Floyd and put his hands on each of the boy's knees, and looked him straight in the eyes.

"You should not be scared of me unless you're tearing up Daven's lawn or fighting with your brother in church. But you already know I'm going to nail you every time for stupid shit like that, which is my job as your father."

"I know, dad, but it's more than that."

"*And* as your father, I would also give my life for you in a heartbeat. No hesitation. That's also my job. Whether or not you accept it is something you have to decide for yourself. Now go finish packing while I have chef make us some dinner. What do you want?"

"Bacon burger and fries."

Hank patted his knees and stood up. "Okay. Consider it done. Pack warmly, it's snowing in Philly."

Floyd lit up. "Really? I've never been…wait, dad, I don't have any snow boots!"

"Oh, shit. Neither do I. Guess we better go shopping and get dinner, then."

"Can we go to Tropical Rainforest Cafe?"

"I don't see why not. Get dressed."

Hank grinned to himself as he hurried down the stairs to find Theo. There was always a way to get Floyd to do what he wanted, one way or the other.

His phone continued to buzz in his pocket unabated as email after email after email came in. He ignored it, and the battery died 20 minutes later.

Urbanes Headquarters, Denver

Harmon eyed the whiskey bottle on the cart in the corner of his office. Must not drink on the job. Must not drink on the job.

Umber had just arrived and was reading his media statement out loud.

It is currently, and always has been, the policy of the FBI to release surveillance tapes to the most interested party first in any investigation. As the victim was one of our employees, we felt it was our duty to take charge of the investigation. Unfortunately, our motives have been-

"No good," said Harmon. "Start over."

"I thought you would say that, so I already have another draft."

It is the legal right of the Urbanes party to-

"No. Start over again."

Umber pulled out another piece of paper. "Right. Thought you'd say that, too."

Hank Bancroft has not been forthcoming about his motivations in obtaining the tapes faster than the law currently provides for. Until it is clear why his rushing into an investigation in which-

"No. No. No," Harmon exclaimed, pounding the desk. "Not even close. Write this down."

Umber whipped out his notepad, and Harmon spoke slowly enough for him get it all.

"The Urbanes Party intends to press integrity charges against Hank Bancroft for misrepresenting our stance on obtaining the surveillance tapes. Our motivation is, and always has been, to complete the investigation as quickly as possible without interference from external parties. We will not comment further, as anything we say at this point would be misconstrued as spin."

Umber looked at him askance.

"Boss, we can't...we can't say this. We can't accuse him of lying, because everything he said was technically true."

"Did you get it all down?"

"Yes, but...but..."

Harmon stood up and put his jacket back on. "Send it out immediately."

US Capitol - Philadelphia

Salome Danby was starting to doze off as she watched the wires come through in a jagged pattern on her specialized news monitor. *Come on, Harmon. I know you're going to do it...just pull the damned trigger already so I can go home and go to bed.*

A jangling alert tone perked her back up, and quickly she pulled up the notification feed. Yep, there it was. And yes, he was not only fanning the flames, but throwing gasoline on them.

She pulled her desk phone over and yanked up the receiver, hitting the number 4 on her speed dial at the same time.

"Stewart, you still at the office? Good. Summon Harmon now. I want him here at 2:00pm Wednesday so we can get him and Hank together. President Rickon himself is planning to spank them both and send them running home with their tails between their legs. Thank you."

CHAPTER FIVE

Bancroft Manor

Finally...

Hank stepped away from the window where he had impatiently been watching and waiting for over an hour for the big black truck to appear across the street in the driveway.

"Hey. Sorry to call so late. You have a minute?"

Daven set down his keys and wallet and braced himself for whatever mood Hank might be in at this particular moment.

"Yes," he answered cautiously. He had all the time in the world for the next 29 days, to be precise.

"Thanks. I have a personal matter to discuss with you. Two, actually."

Oh god. I'm fired, aren't I? Either that or he's going to give me hell for spending so much time with Rupert...or both...

"A personal matter?"

"Yeah. Floyd is really sorry for tearing up your lawn today and wants to come over and apologize. I was wondering if you're available around 9am tomorrow for a few minutes."

"But I told you the grass is fine. Can't even tell."

"You do realize I can see your grass from my bedroom, right? Including the tire tracks."

There was a short pause. "I forgot about that. Anyway, it doesn't matter. The landscapers are coming tomorrow to fix it."

"Fine. He'll be paying their bill with his allowance. And I'm not forcing him to apologize, he actually wants to. So can he come over in the morning?"

"Sure. 9am works. And the second matter?"

Hank took a deep breath. "Listen, do you remember when I told you last month that Floyd got into my study and found out way too much about my past? Well, it freaked him out. I don't know what the hell to do. He's terrified of me, Dav. He's barely talking and acts like I'm going to slit his throat at any moment. Because of one damned photo."

"He's always been afraid of you, Hank. Everyone knows that, except you."

"I do know that, thank you. But this is different." Hank paused to get up and make sure his bedroom door was locked. "I was wondering if...this is stupid. You probably hate me right now, right? And I'm sitting here asking you for favors."

"What do you need?"

"Well, it's a big favor. Feel free to say no. I was wondering if Floyd could spend the next couple of days with you. I think it would do him some good to get away from me for a while."

Daven was confused. "And doing what?"

Hank was becoming a bit rattled by the terseness of Daven's tone and suddenly felt like he was talking to a complete stranger.

"Just being with you. Overnight. I have to travel tomorrow and you know how he is about flying. Tonight he had a panic attack at the mall, and it didn't help that all the paparazzi were following us everywhere. It was pretty bad. Anyway, he gave me such lip afterwards on the way home that I had to…this is…this is really awkward. I don't know why I'm telling you all this."

"I'll do it, Hank, but under one condition."

"What?"

"You have to talk to me about Harmon first. I want to know what you're up to."

Hank sighed heavily. "Dav, no. Forget it."

"Hank, regardless of what you-"

"And what do you mean by *what I'm up to*?' Other than saving your ass, you mean?"

Silence.

Hank continued irritably, "I never would have called you if I thought you'd use Floyd as a bargaining chip. I thought he meant more to you than that. So just forget it. Goodbye, Daven."

"Wait-"

Hank hung up angrily, then laid in bed with his phone on his chest, staring at the ceiling blankly. Sure, he had some serious nerve to pry about Harmon, but what upset him more was that he had basically asked outright if Daven hated him...and Dav hadn't said no.

He hadn't said no , which meant yes.

Hank knew he should apologize for what he'd just said. None of it was true; Daven loved Floyd like a nephew. And he had every right to know why the fight with Harmon had just escalated to new heights. After all, he was still technically his right hand.

But Hank Bancroft was a stubborn man.

Daven kept calling back until Hank blocked his phone number. Then he blocked Rupert's for good measure, and turned over to go to sleep.

A minute later there was a strong knock on his bedroom door that caused him to bolt upright in alarm. No one was allowed to knock on that door, period. That's what the intercom was for. Hank waited in case he had been dreaming, but there was another knock.

"Dad?" It was Theo. Hank jumped up and opened the door.

"What's wrong? Why didn't you use the intercom?"

Theo was upset. "Can you go talk to Floyd?"

"Why? I'm in bed, Theody. It's almost midnight."

"Please. Just make sure he's okay."

Against every ounce of common sense in his body, Hank didn't ask any more questions and followed Theo to Floyd's room.

Floyd was sitting up in his bed, drinking ice water. With one look at his teary face Hank knew something was very wrong. He quickly moved to put a hand on his son's forehead.

"Oh no. You're burning up, buddy."

"I know. I just threw up like five times."

"Your stomach hurt? Like it did last time?"

"Yeah."

"God. Not again. Theody, go get Avery and Brittany. Don't alarm them, just tell them to pull the car to the front door."

"Can I come with you guys?"

"Sure. Hurry up and get dressed."

Palisades Hospital - Los Angeles

Twenty minutes later they arrived at the Palisades Hospital, where Floyd's doctor was thankfully on duty. Since they were the only people there, Floyd was taken in immediately to be seen.

Hank and Theo waited anxiously in the lobby with their guards for what seemed like way too long. Floyd hated being examined in front of anyone, even his own family. He insisted on privacy, and Hank respected that because he was exactly the same way. But it made it all the much harder to wait for the outcome.

"Brittany?" called Hank. "Come here for a second, please."

"Yes, boss?" She moved away from the door and sat down next to him at his invitation.

"I didn't get a chance to thank you for your help at the mall tonight. You and Lucas were invaluable. I was wondering if you would stay with him, if he's admitted."

"Of course."

"Thank you so much. I think that you-"

He didn't get a chance to finish; the doctor called him back to the examining room. It had been almost 90 minutes. Theo was asleep, leaning on Avery. Hank nodded at the man and followed the doctor.

Floyd was laying on the examining table, looking at his dad warily. He had a frightfully pale complexion.

"Is he okay?" Hank asked Dr. Harborough quietly.

"Yes and no," said the pediatrician as she set her clipboard next to Floyd's feet on the bed. "He says he thinks he threw up some blood, and all indications show he was correct. We've been talking about how his anxiety seems to have increased past anything he's felt before."

"Does this mean what I think it means?" asked Hank impatiently.

"I'm afraid so. We'll do one more test to rule out an eosinophilic esophagitis, but I don't think it's that. Looks like we'll have to prescribe him some anxiety meds again."

Hank looked at Floyd, who was now shivering. "Do you have a blanket? And can I talk to him for a minute alone?"

Dr. Harborough reached under into a cabinet and brought out two blankets, which she draped over Floyd herself while Hank just stood there, watching his son closely. The poor kid was still a little green, and his forehead was glistening with sweat.

"Take your time, Mr., Bancroft. Just come out to the desk when you're ready."

The door closed. Floyd was staring at the ceiling now.

"Hey, look at me," Hank started off firmly. They'd been through this a few times before, and his patience was long gone. "How long has your stomach been hurting?"

"Couple of weeks," he mumbled, still staring at nothing.

"And you thought it was okay to go that long without telling me?"

"Mmhmm."

"Ulcers are not a game, Floyd. They're serious business. You promised me last time you wouldn't let it get this far."

Now Floyd looked right at him, expression hard. "It's your fault, so can you at least wait until I feel a little better before you punish me again?"

Hank was shocked. "What? Who said I was going to...okay Floyd, that's it, we got to talk. Man to man. Not here. Home. When you feel better. After I get back from my trip. I can't have you worrying yourself sick over things I did fifteen years ago. This is getting ridiculous."

He got up and left the exam room and went to find the doctor. "If I asked you to admit him again, could you?"

Dr. Harborough nodded. "I was already planning to. Preliminary blood draw shows all sorts of values out of whack. Nothing major, so 48 hours resting and rehydrating should be enough to get him back on track again. And of course I'll refill the fluoxetine. Maybe a little higher dose this time."

"Okay, thanks. He'll need a double room so that his guard can stay with him. Let me go say goodbye."

Hank went back into the room and found Floyd turned all the way around, facing the opposite wall. He picked up the doctor's stool and moved it to where he could sit at eye level with his oldest son. He regretted barking at him a minute ago and made sure to keep his tone calm and kind.

"Theo and I are going to Philadelphia for a couple days. You're going to be admitted now, but we'll pick you up as soon as you're better. Okay?"

Floyd nodded. He didn't mind the hospital at all. It was actually a welcome escape from the life he was growing to hate so much as he got older. This was the fourth time that his ulcers had re-appeared, despite Hank's best efforts to keep the boy calm, happy, and safe.

Hank stroked Floyd's hair. Floyd did not look at him.

"You should go. I'm fine," he said after a moment, pulling back from his father's touch. "Can Theody stay with me?"

"No," replied Hank, pulling the blanket up around Floyd's chin. "Brittany will be here with you. We'll talk in a few days and figure out how to get back to where we were before you saw that photo. I don't want to continue like this. Do you?"

"All I want is for you to quit your job, but you won't listen to me."

"We're not having this conversation again," Hank replied sharply.

"Of course not. It's so much easier to shut me up with your belt."

Hank said nothing more and stood up, knowing that any conversation at this point was useless. Floyd was too wound up to do anything but fight, and any further words would just widen the gap between them.

Theo was awake now and jumped up when Hank returned to the waiting room.

"The ulcers again?"

"I'm afraid so," he responded quietly, giving Theo a quick hug as he did so. "He's going to stay here for a couple of days while you and I go to Philadelphia."

"Can I go talk to him and say goodbye?"

"Yeah, make it quick. Room 4."

Theo rushed back to the exam rooms.

"Hey, jerk."

"What's up, bitch?" replied Floyd automatically as he smiled and struggled to sit up.

"I know you didn't want to go to Philadelphia but this was a little extreme, don't you think?"

Floyd laughed. "Yeah, well you know me. If you're going to fuck something up, do it big."

Theo didn't react. "I asked dad if I could stay here with you but he said no."

"It's okay Theody. Go see the Liberty Bell. Take pictures for me."

"It's just a stupid bell, and it's broken. Have you...are you crying?"

"No. Shut up."

Theo didn't buy it. "Something dad said?"

"I just puked my guts up like five times, Theody. I feel like shit, okay?"

"Okay. Sorry." He sat up on the bed next to his brother. "Lay back down. You're shaking."

Floyd did. "See you in a couple days, then?"

"Yeah. Sorry we're leaving you here."

"It's alright. I don't mind getting away from dad."

Then Theo did something he hadn't done in about three years.

"Move over." He shoved his brother over and laid down next to him.

"Theo! Stop. You're going to push me overboard."

"You're fine." He rested his head on Floyd's shoulder, and Floyd threw his arms around him to hold on for dear life.

"You're too old for this. My ass is hanging off the side," Floyd protested half-heartedly, pulling Theo in tighter all the same. "You want me to sing you nursery rhymes, too?"

"Shut up," Theo giggled.

"So the lab just called and it's definitely *not* esophagitis. So besides the antibiotics, I'm going to go ahead and increase the fluoxetine dose by about 25%. He should still have no side effects at all. Maybe a little drowsiness on the first day."

"Okay. Is he going to have this problem for the rest of his life?"

"Probably. You're not going to like this, but I would like to suggest that you take him to see a child psychologist as soon as possible. That much anxiety in a 15-year old is not even remotely normal."

Hank smiled without humor. "Yeah. We're not exactly a normal family, in case you haven't noticed."

Dr. Harborough shrugged. "You seem way more normal than most of the families I see in here. Theo is the most well-adjusted kid I've ever known, and Floyd would be too, if it wasn't for his crippling fear about your job."

Hank took in a sharp breath. He had told Floyd a million times to never, ever talk about his job. "What? May I ask what he said to you?"

"Yeah, said he can't handle that you're in danger all the time. Surely he's told you that, also?"

"Yes, it's been an ongoing debate. I can't seem to convince him otherwise."

"Well, may I point out that he's not exactly wrong? You don't go anywhere without armed guards, and the poor kid-"

"Thank you doctor. I'll talk to him in a couple of days. What the hell is taking Theo so long?"

Hank stalked back to the exam room and saw his boys lying alongside each other in the bed. Theo was falling asleep, and Floyd put a finger to his lips as his dad came in.

Hank ignored him and laid his hand on Theo's leg. "Up. Let's go."

Floyd protested, "Dad, he-"

"Quiet. Theo, on your feet in five seconds or you're going to get spanked."

"Get up Theo," said Floyd firmly, unwrapping his arms and pushing him up. It was more like fifteen seconds until Theo was out of the bed, but Hank let it go because it was almost 2am and the poor kid was too groggy to obey much faster.

"There's no need to be so mean to him, dad," said Floyd grumpily as he got back under the blanket that Theo had appropriated.

Hank almost snapped at his oldest, but then he relented when he realized how utterly unfair that would be. Instead, he softened his tone.

"Theo, let's get you home and into bed. Go back out to the waiting room for a second."

He left, and Hank walked to the bed to look straight down at his weary son, expression stern but tone as calm as if they were discussing baseball.

"What do you think about coming to work with me when you're feeling better? You can meet everyone, get a better feel for the office. Help me with a few things."

Floyd looked aghast. "Why would I want to do that, dad?"

"Because you seem to think we're some kind of slaughterhouse or something, and that we're running the world, kicking ass, taking names. I'm sorry to say you're going to be really disappointed when you find out how unexciting and normal the organization really is."

"No, thank you."

Hank didn't relent. "And more importantly, you'll see how normal I am, too. Believe it or not, I'm actually a prankster in the office and...shhhh, don't tell anyone, but," he lowered his voice conspiratorially, "your dad is actually *not* a monster. Keep that between us, though." He winked.

Floyd had no intention of giving in. "Right, everything's totally normal. That's why Daven keeps a gun in his drawer and you threatened to send me to boarding school if I get within a mile of the building. Just leave me alone, please."

Hank's response was simply to swallow hard; no possible retort for that one. Floyd had an excellent point. So much for a peace offering.

"Right. Well, I can't argue with you there. I'm going to go. Remember not to talk to anyone about any details of my job. I'll know if you do. Sleep tight. See you Wednesday night."

He turned around and saw Dr. Harborough in the hallway, so he stopped her and spoke in a low voice.

"Who is the best child psychologist in the city?"

———

TWO DAYS LATER..........

PALISADES HOSPITAL

Hank was quite surprised to see Daven sitting worriedly next to Floyd's hospital bed when he arrived back at Palisades. Their eyes locked for a few seconds and Hank's heart leaped a little into his throat, but he pulled his attention away as quickly as he could and focused on Floyd.

"Hey buddy. You feeling well enough to go home?"

"No," mumbled Floyd. Hank was not at all surprised that his son wasn't happy to see him.

"Your doctor thinks you should be discharged. You want to disagree?"

"Yeah. Need to stay here."

Hank got closer to him and felt his forehead. "This isn't a hotel. When they say you're ready to go, we're going. She said she'll be back in half an hour. Promise me you won't fight about it?"

Floyd shrugged noncommittally.

"Need a verbal answer, Floyd."

"I want to stay."

Hank pushed his irritation aside. "We'll see. I'm going to go to the cafeteria and grab a snack real quick. Haven't had dinner yet. Daven, want to join me?"

Dav looked up from where he'd been studying his fingernails, then he leapt to his feet. "That'd be great." He looked over to Floyd, who had his eyes shut again. "See you later, Floyd-o."

"Bye Uncle Dav."

They walked down the hall in silence, a guard in front and behind them. Daven then veered off to the left, but Hank called after him.

"Dav? What are you doing?"

"I'm...leaving? Parked out this door." He pointed behind him.

A group of women at a nursing station was watching them, so Hank forced himself to sound cheerful. "Can you join me for a quick bite in the cafeteria, first?"

"Uh...sure."

They went, still walking in silence, and sat down in a private booth after grabbing snacks and water. Avery was hovering at first, but Hank shooed him away.

"I'm sorry, Hank," blurted Daven, a little desperately. "But Floyd called me and begged me to come, and we couldn't reach you because you were in the air. He tried to call you after you landed but it seemed like your phone is dead. And…it seems my number might be blocked.”

“It is,” replied Hank calmly.

Daven looked as if he was about to say something about that, but changed his mind. “Okay. I couldn’t just say no to Floyd, so I’ve been here about 4 hours. He was asleep most of the time. I think he just needed a familiar face to watch over him, with Brittany being so new and all. He didn’t say much of anything, but you’ll be happy to know he managed to apologize for the grass incident before dozing off.”

“Good.” Hank took a bite of an apple slice. “Did he say anything about me at all?”

Daven looked incredibly uncomfortable all of a sudden. “He did, and I’ll tell you if you really want to know.”

“Do I want to know?”

“No.”

Hank grimaced. “Okay. Never mind. Thank you for coming. I know it meant a lot to him.”

"And I'll leave as soon as...wait. What?" Daven cocked his head sideways. "I thought you would be...you're not upset?"

"Not at all." Now Hank chugged down the rest of his coffee, but said nothing more as he wondered why the hell he was drinking coffee at 11pm. There was a long, awkward silence as he pondered the question without any answer except that he was possibly a little jet lagged.

"Ok, well...you're welcome," said Daven eventually, as he played with his tie. The ultimate sign of nervousness.

Hank finished his apple and then leaned forward a little bit, fully conscious of all the eyes on him in the cafeteria. "Trust me when I say that you visiting Floyd without my consent is the very least of my concerns right now. I would have said yes anyway, had you managed to reach me. So don't worry about it."

"Oh. That's good to know. I would hate to think that you didn't want me to see him anymore. You know, considering I treat him as a mere *bargaining chip* and all."

Hank's expression didn't change. "Can we talk business for a moment? Preferably without the passive aggressive commentary."

Says the king of passive aggressive behavior. "Of course," Daven murmured, feeling rather ashamed of his jibe all of a sudden, no matter how well-deserved it was.

Hank signaled Avery over and asked him apologetically to refill his coffee mug. As soon as the man stepped away, Hank took a deep breath. "Before I say anything else, I just need to know if you're really planning to come back to the office in a month, or if you...you know, let's just say I wouldn't blame you if you didn't want to work for me anymore."

Daven looked puzzled. "Do you even have to ask?"

"Yeah, I do, actually. Because I honestly don't know what's going on in your head right now."

"You know how you can find out? Stop shutting me out and talk to me."

Hank could see that Daven was entirely sincere, so he plunged forward. "Okay, good point. I'm sure Floyd told you I've been in Philadelphia. I got summoned there under the pretense of meeting with Stewart to get berated for publicly throwing the FBI and Harmon under the bus. Turns out Harmon was summoned for his own response, and we were hauled in together before the president himself to get our asses kicked for embarrassing the politics community at large."

Daven was completely stunned. "Holy shit, Hank," was all he could say.

Hank added, "Yeah. There's more. We really need to talk, but not here. Can you come to my house tomorrow night?"

"What about Rupert?" Daven asked after a moment. "If this is a serious business matter, he should hear about it as well."

"I don't disagree with you, but...honestly, your opinions carry more weight at the moment. Especially after how much he fought me over that last press release."

"I don't agree at all, Hank" Daven responded, even though he was secretly flattered. "If we're to rebuild trust between the three of us, we need to get past these differences in opinions and just talk to each other plainly in the future. Otherwise..." *this will all happen again....*

Hank nodded. "Okay, agreed. Since his family eats dinner at 6:30, let's meet at 5. I'll leave work a little early and you guys can meet me at the new house."

Daven smiled. "Great. I've been wanting to see it."

"The electricity and water was just turned on yesterday, so I'm rather eager to see it myself. The security gate uses fingerprints, but the bypass code is 40774077."

Of course it was. Hank was a huge fan of M*A*S*H. And there was another reason he wanted to go to that house, too: the long driveway was completely private and solidly gated. Although the top of the house was visible from the street, no one would be able to see any cars that were coming and going, never mind any activity at the front door. For that reason alone, Hank could not wait to move in.

"Okay." Daven wanted to ask Hank to unblock his phone number, but it was perhaps too soon for that. Maybe he would even do it on his own.

"There's one more thing, Dav, before I go back to Floyd."

"Yes?"

"I just...the harsh things I've said to you lately. I'm not even sorry. I'm having some serious trust issues right now. With you, with Rupe, with my guards. With Stewart. With my own sons. Honestly, I don't even trust myself at the moment. This whole thing has just kind of shattered me, and I'm resentful and unhappy, and...a lot of things. But I'm really trying to work through it and get us back to where we were before. I need your patience and understanding."

Daven nodded. "Understood. In the spirit of being completely honest, can I say something a little harsh in return?"

"Sure, why not."

"You've been scaring the shit out of the same people you claim not to trust anymore, Hank. I don't think that's a coincidence."

Hank looked like he hadn't heard correctly. "I...what?"

"You heard me correctly. I would like to posit that maybe your trust issues with everyone else are happening because *they're* starting not to trust *you*. Not your motivations, of course, but your impulsiveness and need to always have the last word. it's dangerous."

Hank was flabbergasted. "That's...that's what you call a *little* harsh?"

Daven took a deep gulp of his own water. "I call it the truth. And if I didn't care about you, I wouldn't tell you this outright and risk you shutting me out forever: you should have never thrown the FBI and Harmon into the fire on national television. It was vain, and aggressive, and altogether indefensible. The Hank Bancroft I want to work for knows when he's getting too smart for his own good."

Hank smiled a little. "Too smart, huh?"

Daven did not smile back. "Yes."

"Even though I got exactly what I wanted?"

"You did? You got the tapes?"

Hank winked. "No. Even better. Harmon was put on a 90-day probation. One more misstep and he's gone."

"But...doesn't that apply to you, too?" Daven was appalled.

"Nope. I just got a warning." Hank grinned. "My first one. Harmon already had two, so that's why I baited him at the press conference. Knew he couldn't resist shooting himself in the foot and earning that final warning."

Daven almost asked if he had planned this all out from the very beginning, from the moment they learned of the murder, as Rupert had said. It now seemed incredibly likely. But he stopped himself when he realized he didn't *really* want to know the answer to that.

An ill omen seized Daven's heart like a claw grip, and he realized he no longer trusted the man who was sitting in front of him, calmly drinking his third cup of coffee at midnight and smiling to himself victoriously.

CHAPTER SIX

Los Angeles

"Okay, wait, Hank...so you're saying you *purposely* earned yourself a warning in order to see if you might be able to take Harmon down with you?"

Rupe was carefully aghast, and Hank sighed as they all climbed the stairs up to the second floor of Hank's new house after just having touring the mostly-finished kitchen.

"Don't be so dramatic. It was a calculated risk to make him behave and focus on other things besides all this back-and-forth aggression between our parties."

Aggression that you started, thought Daven.

"Oh, I like this big landing," Rupert cooed. "Lots of natural light."

"I was going to carpet this area, but it will be hard to keep clean with all the foot traffic. My sitting room is up this staircase," he said, pointing. "It's the only room with furniture so far."

He turned around and yelled down to Lucas, who was still wandering around on the first floor.

"Lucas! We'll be up in my sitting room, all is well. Can you wait in the car, please, or in the pool house?"

"I'll wait in the car, boss," he called back.

"You can see Dav's house from here, too," Rupert laughed as they reached the top of the stairs.

Daven looked out the window. "Just the roof. Guess I won't be sunbathing naked up there anymore."

Normally Hank would make some kind of inappropriate homoerotic joke at this point, but he said nothing, which was somewhat disappointing to the other men.

There were only two chairs in the room - still plastic-wrapped - so after Hank closed the door, he sat on the broad window sill while Dav and Rupe plopped themselves down onto the squeaky, slippery chairs.

"Sorry," he said. "I would take off the plastic, but we still need to paint in here."

"So, you were actually in the same room with Harmon when this all went down with the president?" asked Rupert, whose expression was darkening by the second.

"Yup. Standing right next to him. Alright gents, get comfy. I'm going to tell you everything that happened from the moment we touched down in Philly...So I get to the waiting room, which they call the *antechamber* because they're so full of themselves, and guess who's sitting there looking as smug as a cat in a box? Harmon himself."

Urbanes Headquarters, Denver

"So I just looked straight at him and said, good day, Hank. I'm glad to see you've gained weight since we were last together. I was a little worried about your health for a while."

"So I just laughed. I've gained maybe five pounds since then, all muscle."

"Hank was so pissed. You should have seen his face."

"I got up to shake Harmon's hand and he immediately came over to me and acted like we've been best buddies for fifteen years."

"I didn't think he'd talk to me after the insult, which is what I wanted, but he got up and started glad-handing me until I had to move away. Twice. No sense of personal space whatsoever. He must drive Rupert and Daven nuts."

"So I tried my best to make him as uncomfortable as possible. Taking his hand and then wiping my nose and shaking his hand again. You know how he is with that germophobia. I just kept closing in. And he kept backing up, and I'm trying my damndest not to laugh the whole time."

"Thankfully President Rickon quickly came out and called us in, looking like he just sucked on a lemon, as usual. Salome and Stewart were seated on either side of him."

"They didn't even ask us to sit. Felt like I was in the principal's office again, waiting to get my ass beat."

"The first thing he says is that we have shamed our parties, ourselves, and our constituents in general. Then he gives us a

copy of our press releases and has us read them out loud to the entire room."

"Then we had to switch and read each other's press releases to each other. I'm still trying not to laugh. And there was this really long, uncomfortable silence as the president pulled out two books from under his desk. Taking his time flipping to pages he wants."

"And he hands them to us and makes us read out the entire code of conduct that Hank and I both had to agree to and sign before the parties could be legitimized by President Hannigan."

"The entire damned thing. Simultaneously. Every freakin' word. It took an hour. I had to piss half the time."

"We finally get to the end and then he pulls out the appendix to that agreement, which lists all of the consequences for every possible violation of the code of conduct. Makes us read that one, too, in full."

"So basically for 90 minutes we're doing this, and I can tell Harmon has to piss too because he's getting all fidgety and looks approximately as annoyed as I am."

"I seriously had to take a shit at this point. And for some reason Hank thinks the whole damned thing is hilarious."

"Then Salome asked us if there was anything we did not understand, so that she could provide clarification. We both said no, so she handed us a pen and we had to sign the book again with the current date."

"The president proceeds to remind us that per the terms of our charters, he is technically our boss, and has the power to take disciplinary action if needed...which is needed now, he adds."

"Up to and including removal from our positions. He then issued an order for us to speak to each other every single day for ten minutes at 10am."

"We each have to hand write out the entire code of conduct, terms & consequences, and our own charters, and submit them with 90 days."

"If we don't do it, we lose our jobs. Period."

"Then he issued me a final warning, and gave Hank his first warning. Then he dismissed us."

"And that was it. I ran to the bathroom on one side of the lobby and Harmon ran to the other one. And when we came out, we were told a car was waiting for us."

"The nail in the coffin came when we were made to share a car back to the airport, and there was a ton of traffic on 95 so it took forever to get there."

"We didn't talk at first, until I asked him if he was still friends with Lester Boyd. Turns out they're still in touch. Lester's some kind of school teacher now in Virginia. That surprised the hell out of me, to say the least. Didn't seem he was that type. Anyway, at least we found that common ground to talk about."

"On the way there, Hank asked me about Lester Boyd. I knew they had some kind of falling out ten years ago, but I didn't know they were that close. So I just said he was a teacher. Didn't mention what kind."

"And then we got to the airport. Theo just about wet his pants when he saw us get out of the car together, and my guards probably did, too, but there was no further drama."

Daven looked surprised. "You actually talked about Lester Boyd? Your college roommate who almost shot you the last time you saw each other?"

Rupert's eyebrows raised way up. "Wait, what? I haven't heard this particular story. Do tell."

"Yeah, thanks for the reminder, Dav." Hank rolled his eyes. "As you know, we parted ways after Harmon asked him to join the Urbanes. Lester thought that's where I was headed, too. In the same night, he learned I was chosen to run the Seditionists *and* that we'd been banging the same woman...well, let's just say we had a really big fight about it, among other things. Anyway. He ended up getting married to one of my old girlfriends later on. I'll leave it at that."

"Sordid. So now you and Harmon are BFFs now, huh?" asked Rupert with a thin smile.

Hank frowned. "Hardly. But I think we came to somewhat of a truce by the time we got to the airport. There's something else, though, and it's the reason I asked you to come over."

Rupe moaned. "Oh god, what now?"

Hank cleared his throat. "He told me this morning on the phone that Colbert suspects Janet was a double agent. Then he said their double agents are so untrustworthy that as of yesterday they're not going to use them anymore, after one went radio silent for a week. He asked me to do the same, in order to *maintain good relations*. What do you think of that?"

Rupert blurted right away, "I think he's lying."

"Absolutely," agreed Daven. "Don't trust him, Hank. Not for a heartbeat. He may not be *employing* them, strictly speaking, but he'll get inside information in other ways."

Hank nodded. "The thought occurred to me afterwards that maybe I should have asked Harmon if that agent was responsible for the calls that got you guys in trouble."

Daven shook his head. "He has no reason to tell you that."

"He fired him for a reason, Dav. And he last heard from him at Christmas, or right before. I don't think that's a coincidence. He wouldn't have mentioned it other-" He paused as a low, jangly noise emanated from his backside. "Hang on, my phone's ringing."

Hank pulled it out of his pocket and was astonished to see Harmon's cell phone number and name in the caller ID. He managed to keep a straight face somehow and stood up to walk just outside the door, then answered the phone cheerfully.

"Hey Theody, what's up?"

"Hank, it's...it's Harmon," said the curt voice on the other end.

"Oh yeah, I know," Hank relied casually. His heart was pounding in his ears.

"Ah, I see. You're not alone."

"Nope."

"I'll make this quick, then. On our call this morning you asked me if I would consider turning the name of our double agent over to you. The one I just had Colbert fire for going silent on us for a week."

Hank's throat went dry. "Yeah, I remember."

"I will tell you his name 24 hours from now if you do me a favor."

Hank felt a bit dizzy and sick suddenly.

"Why exactly are you calling to tell me this now? Could this not have waited?"

Hank heard Harmon take a deep breath. "I needed an unrecorded line. On tomorrow's 10am call, I'm going to ask you if Janet was a double agent. Colbert is going to be with me, listening silently. I need you to not fight with me about it, and just say no. Even if she was."

"Uh. Why?"

"I can't tell you right now. You'll have to trust me."

"Ah. The answer is no, I won't do you that favor. Don't ask me again, Theody."

Hank hung up, rattled to the core. *Fuck...*

"Hank? Everything okay?" Rupe asked in alarm as he saw Hank's flushed cheeks a moment later.

"Yeah, I'm...it's been a long day. Let's get out of here and go back to the house for dinner. I can't think straight anymore."

"Hank, we haven't even-" they both began.

"Let's go anyway."

He hurried down the stairs while Daven and Rupert looked at each other with wide eyes.

"That wasn't Theo," whispered Rupert. "Did you notice the ringtone?"

"No. Why?"

"It was the 'Halloween' theme song."

Dav was still puzzled. "Okay, so..?"

"It's kind of an inside joke. That's the ringtone Hank uses for Harmon. And only for Harmon. I'm telling you, that was *not* Theo."

"What the hell..." whispered Daven.